Franklin B. Hough

Proceedings of a Convention of Delegates from Several of the New-England States

held at Boston, August 3-9, 1780 - to advise on affairs necessary to promote the most vigorous prosecution of the war

Franklin B. Hough

Proceedings of a Convention of Delegates from Several of the New-England States
held at Boston, August 3-9, 1780 - to advise on affairs necessary to promote the most vigorous prosecution of the war

ISBN/EAN: 9783337367688

Printed in Europe, USA, Canada, Australia, Japan

Cover: Foto ©Andreas Hilbeck / pixelio.de

More available books at **www.hansebooks.com**

PROCEEDINGS

OF A

Convention of Delegates

FROM SEVERAL OF THE

·NEW-ENGLAND STATES,

Held at Boston, August 3–9, 1780,

TO ADVISE ON AFFAIRS

NECESSARY TO PROMOTE THE MOST

VIGOROUS PROSECUTION OF THE WAR,

AND TO PROVIDE FOR

A GENEROUS RECEPTION OF

OUR FRENCH ALLIES.

EDITED FROM AN ORIGINAL MANUSCRIPT RECORD IN THE
NEW YORK STATE LIBRARY,

WITH

An Introduction and Notes.

By FRANKLIN B. HOUGH.

PREFACE.

THE following Journal is printed from a Manufcript Copy of the Proceedings of the Convention to which it relates, that was tranfmitted to George Clinton, Governor of New York, by. Thomas Cufhing, Prefident of the Convention, with the Defign of enlifting his favorable Attention and Aid in the Meafures recommended.

Although alluded to in the cotemporary Correfpondence of their Day, we have never feen them in Print. In placing the Record of thefe Proceedings within the Reach of public Libraries, and Collectors of American Hiftory, we feel the Affur-

ance that the patriotic Spirit and Tone
that they evince, will leave an Impreſſion
favorable to the Parties concerned, and
afford additional Proofs of the earneſt
and heroic Determination that actuated
the Founders of our Republic.

But theſe Papers derive a ſtill greater
Intereſt, from the Evidence they preſent
of the Conviction of their Framers in the
Neceſſity of a ſtill ſtronger Bond of Union
among the States, than could be ſecured
by the Articles of Union and Confederation then under Diſcuſſion, and already
adopted by moſt of the States. The
Members of this Convention declared
their Belief, that the Powers of Congreſs
ſhould be more clearly aſcertained and
defined, and that the important national
Concerns of the United States ſhould be
under the Superintendency and Direction
of one ſupreme Head. This Theory was

not realized until the Adoption of the
Federal Conftitution, nearly nine Years
afterwards; and the Bofton Convention
of Auguft, 1780, may, we believe, be
regarded as the firft public Expreffion of
Opinion, by a deliberative Body, in Favor
of fuch a Meafure.   They urged the Adoption of the Articles of Confederation, as
effential to the public Good; yet, as
thefe Articles did not provide the fupreme
executive Head, which they believed to
be neceffary for the national Welfare, it is
evident that they regarded them as falling
fhort of the Wants of the Government,
although probably at the Time the beft
that could be fecured.

We may therefore be permitted to offer
thefe Proceedings, as a commendable Record of Patriotifm and Forethought on
the Part of thofe who participated in
them, and the Refolutions reported, as

among the earlieſt Movements towards
the eſtabliſhment of a Form of Government analogous to that which went into
Effect on the fourth of March, 1789;
and their Authors as entitled to an
honorable Claim for the Honors due to
Pioneers in the Formation of our National
Union.

F. B. H.

INTRODUCTION.

THE Condition of our public Affairs, in the Summer of 1780, had become greatly embarraſſed by the Decline in Value of the Bills of Credit, that had been Iſſued in the early Part of the War, and which had fallen to a merely nominal Value. The Coſt of Tranſportation and Supplies for the Army had increaſed in a proportional Degree. The Pay of Officers and Soldiers no longer proved adequate to meet their own Wants and the preſſing Demands of their Families. Supplies could no longer be procured with this Money by voluntary Sale, and vigorous Meaſures became neceſſary to ſuſtain the military Operations of the Campaign, by other Means than thoſe employed with a full Treaſury and a national Credit unimpaired.

Although, with the Exception of the more fouthern Colonies, the Enemy at this Period had made no confiderable Progrefs in their Efforts at Conqueft, and only held a narrow Tract at a few Points along the Coaft, as the Fruit of their five Years Struggle, they had of late evinced confiderable Activity. Incurfions along the northern and weftern Frontiers became frequent, withdrawing a confiderable Force from the Continental Army and the State Militia for garrifoning the Pofts in the Interior, and refulting in ferious Lofs from the Deftruction of Provifions, and the Neglect of Agriculture, which the exifting War occafioned.

The Refources of the Country were becoming rapidly exhaufted, but the Afpirations for that Independence which the Colonies had afferted were never more earneft than at this Period. The Condition of public Affairs at this Crifis will be beft underftood from the following Letter of General Wafhington to Congrefs, and the Correfpondence and Circulars that follow :

LETTER FROM GENERAL WASHINGTON TO CONGRESS.

Head-Quarters, Orangetown,
Auguſt 17th, 1780.*

Gentlemen,

We are now arrived at the middle of Auguſt; if we are able to undertake any Thing in this Quarter this Campaign, our Operations muſt commence in leſs than a Month from this, or it will be abſolutely too late. It will then be much later than were to be wiſhed, and with all the Exertions that can be made, we ſhall probably be greatly ſtraitened in Time.

But I think it my Duty to inform you, that our Proſpects of operating diminiſh in Proportion as the Effects of our Applications to the reſpective States unfold; and I am ſorry to add, that we have every Reaſon to apprehend, we ſhall not be in a Condition at all to undertake any Thing deciſive.

The Completion of our Continental Battalions to their full Eſtabliſhment of five hundred and four Rank and File, has been uniformly and juſtly held up as the Baſis of offenſive Operations.

---

* This Letter does not occur among the Writings of General Waſhington, edited by Mr. Sparks, and we are not aware that it has ever before been printed.

B

How far we have fallen fhort of this the following State of the Levies received, and of the prefent Deficiency will fhow.

By a Return to the 11th Inftant we have received from,

	Rank and File.
New Hampfhire, - - - -	457
Maffachufetts, - - - -	2,898
Rhode Ifland, - - - - -	502
Connecticut, - - - -	1,356
New York, - - - - -	283
New Jerfey, - - - -	165
Pennfylvania, - - - - -	482
	6,143

The Deficiencies of the Battalions, from a Return of the 12th, allowing for the Levies fince arrived to the 16th are:

	Rank and File.
Of New Hampfhire, 3 Battalions, - -	248
Of Maffachufetts, including Jackfon's adopted, 16 Battalions, - - -	3,514
Of Rhode Ifland, 2 do., - - -	198
Of Connecticut, including Webb's Battalion adopted, - - - -	1,866
Of New York, 5 Battalions, - - -	1,234
New Jerfey, 3 do., - - -	569
Pennfylvania, 4 do., - - -	2,768

In the Whole, 10,397 Rank and File.

If the Amount of thefe Deficiences, and the detached Corps neceffary on the Frontier, and at particular Pofts, be deducted and a proper Allowance made for the ordinary Cafualties, and for the extra Calls upon the Army for Waggoners, Artificers, &c., it will be eafy to conceive how inadequate our operating Force muft be to any capital Enterprife againft the Enemy. It is indeed barely fufficient for Defence.

Hitherto all the Militia for three Months that have taken the Field under my Orders have been about

700 from New Hampfhire.

1,700 from Maffachufetts.

800 from New York.

500 from New Jerfey.

A Part of the eaftern Militia has been detained to affift our Allies at Rhode Ifland, and will fhortly march to join the Army. But from all the Information I have, the Number of Militia will fall as far fhort of the Demands as the Continental Troops; and from the flow Manner in which the latter have for fome Time paft come in, I fear we have had nearly the Whole we are to expect.

In the Article of Provifions, our Profpects

are equally unfavourable. We are now fed on a precarious Supply from Day to Day. The Commiſſary, from what has been done in the ſeveral States, ſo far from giving Aſſurances of a Continuance of this Supply, ſpeaks in the moſt diſcouraging Terms; as you will perceive by the incloſed Copy of a Letter of the 15th, in which he propoſes the ſending back the Pennſylvania Militia, who were to aſſemble at Trenton the 12th, on the Principle of a Failure of Supplies.

As to Forage, and Tranſportation, our Proſpects are ſtill worſe. Theſe have lately been procured by military Impreſs — a Mode too violent, une-qual, oppreſſive and conſequently odious to the People, to be long practiced with Succeſs.

In this State of Things, Gentlemen, I leave it to your own Judgment to determine how little it will be in my Power to anſwer the Public Expectation unleſs more competent Means can be — and without Delay, put into my Hands. From the Communications of the General and Admiral of our Allies, the Second Diviſion, without ſome very unfavorable Contrary, will in all Probability arrive before the Time men-tioned as the ultimate Period for commencing our Operations. I ſubmit it to you, whether it will not be advifable, immediately to lay before the feveral States a View of Circumftances at this Juncture, in Confequence of which they may take their Meafures.

I have the Honor to be, with the greateft Refpect and Efteem,

Gentlemen,

Your moft obedient Serv't,

GEO. WASHINGTON.

N. B. The Return of the Rhode Ifland Recruits is of the laft of July. More may have fince joined. There is a Body of Connecticut State Troops and Militia employed in preparing Fafcines, &c., on the Sound.

CIRCULAR LETTER OF COMMITTEE OF CONGRESS.

[Referred to in the Meffage of Gov. Clinton, given in the Appendix.]

In Committee of Congrefs,
Camp Tappan, Auguft 16, 1780.

(CIRCULAR.)

Sir,

Enclofed you will receive Copy of a Letter of the 18th Inftant from the Commiffary General.

Circumftanced as our Army at Prefent is, the

Information contained in this Letter becomes truly alarming. It requires the utmoſt Attention of the Officers, together with all the Neceſſaries and even Comforts of Life, to render the Service acceptable to Recruits; and as the greateſt Part of the Army at Preſent conſiſts of that Claſs of Men, if the Time ſhould unhappily arrive when we will be reduced to the Neceſſity of putting them on half Allowance of Proviſions or probably have none to give them, the Conſequence muſt be, that theſe Men unaccuſtomed to endure this Species of Diſtreſs, and not brought to that State of Diſcipline which can give their Officers that Controul over them, they have acquired over the old Soldiers, muſt revolt at the Idea of tamely ſubmitting to a Service, when diveſted as they are of every Privilege the Soldiers of all Armies are entitled to, and are furniſhed with, they cannot receive even the Means of Subſiſtence. If reduced to the Extremity I have juſt men-tioned, and an irreconcilable Diſguſt ſhould once take Place among theſe Men, and Deſertions (or perhaps Something worſe) begin, the Contagion will, beyond a Doubt pervade the whole Army. For it is not to be expected that the few old Soldiers now remaining will be diſpoſed to go on, enduring the Calamities they have fo often experienced, when they find others equally bound with themfelves and who have as yet had none of thefe Difficulties to encounter, manifefting fo refractory a Spirit at what they conceive to be Trifles, compared with their own Sufferings. Should fuch an Event take Place, the Train of ruinous Confequences that will inevitably enfue, muft at once ftrike you fo obvioufly, as to render unneceffary my entering into a Detail of them.

We do therefore earneftly requeft you, Sir, that the Officers of your State, appointed to procure and forward the Supplies, may be called on, in the moft urgent Manner, to give their utmoft Attention to the important Bufinefs of keeping the Army regularly fupplied with your Quota of the Articles that has been affigned to your State, as you muft plainly perceive what Embarraffment the leaft Remiffion on the Part of the States or any of them muft throw us into: For it muft be remembered, that the monthly Supplies are no more than what is barely neceffary for the Confumption of the Army in that Time.

It is true that the Army at Prefent does not amount to the Numbers on which the Eftimate

was made, but as the Men are daily coming in,
we are to fuppofe that the Complement of Men
will be made up by the End of this Month.
But at all Events, it is incumbent on us to be
provided to anfwer the largeft Demands that can
be made on us.

It is not only the immediate Supplies of the
Army, that the Committee would wifh to call
your Attention to, but likewife the Neceffity there
is of the greateft Punctuality in furnifhing the
Supplies agreeable to the Requifitions that have
been heretofore made, to prevent in future, Alarms
of this Nature, and our giving you further Trouble
on the Subject.

I have the Honor to be,
with the higheft Refpect
Your Excellency's
Moft obedient Servant,
In behalf of the Committee,
JNO. MATTHEWS.

His Excellency,
George Clinton, Efq.

LETTER FROM EPHRAIM BLAINE, COMMISSARY GE-
NERAL OF PURCHASES, TO A COMMITTEE OF
CONGRESS.

Tappan, 15th Auguſt, 1780.

Gentlemen,

The Army daily increaſing, and a Declenſion
of Supplies, makes me dread the moſt fatal Con-
ſequences. Our Continental Magazines are quite
exhauſted, in every Part of the United States,
and no other Method of procuring Proviſions,
but through the reſpective States. The Requiſi-
tion of Congreſs upon the States was calculated
to ſupply the American Army and its Dependen-
cies. That made by your honorable Committee
was to anſwer the Demands of the Campaign,
agreeable to a Calculation for that Purpoſe. Many
of the States have done little, others are moving
ſlowly, and thoſe who are uſing their utmoſt
Exertions will fall ſhort of the Supplies required.
I have this Day received Advice that there is
little Flour at Elk, Chriſtana, and the Communication to Trenton, of Courſe the Supply of
that Article muſt fail. The States who are called
upon for Cattle are alſo tardy. The Army now
fed from Hand to Mouth, (on the Receivals of
this Day depend the Iſſues of tomorrow). In

C

this critical Situation is an Army, which confumes twenty five thoufand Rations daily, two thirds of which are new Levies, not accuftomed to the Hardfhips of the Field, or Want of Provifions in Camp. Under thefe Circumftances two Days Failure of Supplies might be attended with difagreeable Events, which might not be in the Power of his Excellency the Commander-in-Chief to remedy. Have therefore to requeft you to ufe every poffible Meafure with Congrefs, and the executive Authorities of the refpective States, to pay due Attention to your Demands. A Neglect of which will be a Diffolution of the Army.

In the former Syftem of the Commiffariat, all Perfons employed in the Department were, by an Order of Congrefs, exempted from militia Duty and Fine. The Perfons employed in Philadelphia are all claffed and fined, without they render perfonal Service. My Cafhier, who has the principal Direction of my Office when abfent, the Receival of all Letters and Settlement of Accounts—but one Clerk to affift in tranfacting the whole of my Bufinefs, feveral other Perfons employed as Receivers and Drovers of Cattle— thefe Perfons have fcarcely a daily Subfiftence;

and without they are exempted from thefe Fines, which they are not able to pay, I muft be under the Neceffity of fhutting up my Office, and all Bufinefs ceafe. One of my Clerks is fined four thoufand Dollars, the other eleven hundred Pounds. Have not been informed what other Perfons have to pay. I requeft your Anfwer to this Matter, as they have wrote me if the Public do not exempt them from Payment of their Fines, Neceffity will oblige them to quit my Office.

You may reft affured of my utmoft Endeavours to keep up Supplies, but prefent Profpects are not favorable; and believe every Endeavour will prove ineffectual without the States ufe four Fold Exertions.

I have the Honor to be,
        With every Sentiment of Efteem,
                Your moft obedient, humble Serv't,
                        Eph. Blaine, C. G. P.

    The Honorable
Committee of Congrefs.

LETTER FROM GOVERNOR CLINTON TO EPHRAIM
BLAINE.

Poughkeepfie, 18th Auguft, 1780.

Sir,

Your Letter of the 9th Inftant is this Moment
delivered me. Every Exertion making for col-
lecting the fpecific Supplies required of this State.
The Moment this is accomplifhed, there will not
be the leaft Objection againft the Agent for this
State extending his Purchafes as much farther as
the Refources of the State will admit of, and the
public Service may require. But as fuch extra
Purchafes muft be made at the Expenfe of the
United States, and under the Direction of the
Commiffary General, it will be neceffary that he
fhould have your Order for the Purpofe; without
which, however prefling the Demand, I am not
authorized to direct him to exceed the Requifi-
tion made of [on] the State.

Should he receive your Orders you may rely
on any Affiftance in my Power to render his
Appointments as extenfively ufeful as poffible.

I am, Sir,

Your moft obedient Serv't,

G. CLINTON.

CIRCULAR LETTER OF COMMITTEE OF CONGRESS.

In Committee of Congreſs,
Camp Tappan, Auguſt 19, 1780.

(CIRCULAR.)

Sir,

When America ſtood alone againſt one of the moſt powerful Nations of the Earth, the Spirit of Liberty ſeemed to animate her Sons to the nobleſt Exertions, and each Man cheerfully contributed his Aid in Support of her deareſt Rights. When the Hand of Tyranny ſeemed to bear its greateſt Weight on this devoted Country, their Virtue and Perſeverance appeared moſt conſpicuous, and roſe ſuperior to every Difficulty. If then, ſuch Patriotiſm manifeſted itſelf throughout all Ranks and Orders of Men amongſt us, ſhall it be ſaid at this Day, this early Day of our Enfranchiſement and Independence, that America has grown tired of being free? Let us, Sir, but for a Moment take a retroſpective View of our then Situation, and compare it with the preſent, and draw ſuch Deductions from the Premiſes as every reaſonable Man, or ſet of Men, ought to do.

In the early Stage of this glorious Revolution

we ftood alone.   We had neither Army, military
Stores, Money, or in fhort any of thofe Means
which are requifite to authorize a Refiftance.
The Undertaking was phyfically againft us.   But
Americans abhorred the very Idea of Slavery.
Therefore repofing the Righteoufnefs of their
Caufe in the Hands of the Supreme Difpofer of
all human Events, they boldly ventured to defy
the Vengeance of a Tyrant, and either preferve
their Freedom inviolate to themfelves and Pof-
terity, or perifh in the Attempt.   This was the
Situation and Temper of the People of this
Country in the Beginning of this Controverfy.
At this Day, America is in ftrict Alliance with
one of the firft Nations of the Earth, for Mag-
nanimity, Power and Wealth, and whofe Affairs
are conducted by the ableft Statefmen, with a
Prince at their Head, who hath juftly acquired
the Title of the Protector of the Rights of Mankind.   A refpectable Fleet and Army of our Ally
are already arrived amongft us, and a confiderable
Reinforcement is hourly expected, which, when
arrived, will give us a decided Superiority in thefe
Seas—the Whole to cooperate with the Force
of this Country againft the common Enemy.
Another powerful Nation (Spain) though not

immediately allied with us, yet in fighting her own, she is daily fighting the Battles of America, from whence almost every Advantage is derived to us that could be produced in a State of Alliance. An Army we now have in the Field, Part of whom are Veterans, equal to any the oldest established Nations can boast. Our Militia, from a five Years War, are become enured to Arms. You have at the Head of your Army a General whose Abilities as a Soldier and Worth as a Citizen stand confessed, even by the Enemies of his Country. Our Officers of all Ranks are fully equal to the Duties of their respective Stations. Military Stores are within our Reach. Our Money, tho' not as reputable as that of other Nations, with proper Attention, we have Reason to expect, will shortly emerge from its present embarrassed State, and become as useful as ever.

Now, Sir, from a comparative View of our Circumstances at the Beginning, and at this Day, how much more eligible, how much more pleasing and important must the latter appear than the 'former, to every dispassionate Man! Then shall we leave to future Generations to · say, shall we at Present commit ourselves to the World to exclaim, that when Providence had

benignly put into our Hands the moſt eſſential
Means of obtaining by one deciſive Blow the
ineſtimable Prize we had been contending for,
it was loſt — diſgracefully loſt, for Want of
proper Exertions on our Part ? That Avarice,
Luxury and Diſſipation had ſo enervated the
boaſted Sons of American Freedom, that rather
than forego their preſent Eaſe, and wanton Plea-
ſures, they would tamely, cowardly ſubmit to
the Loſs of their Country, and their Liberty,
and become thoſe abject Slaves, which their
generous Natures but a few Years before would
have revolted at the very Idea.

Theſe Reflections ariſe, Sir, from the extraor-
dinary Backwardneſs of ſome States, and great
Deficiences in others, in ſending the Men into
the Field that was required of them, near three
Months ago, and ought to have joined the Army
fifty Days paſt, and an Apprehenſion, that from
this Torpitude America has forgot ſhe is contending for Liberty and Independence, and that
the good Intentions of our generous Ally will be
totally fruſtrated by our unpardonable Remiſſneſs.
Our former Letters to the States have been full on
this very important Subject, and we are concerned
to be driven to the Neceſſity of Reiteration ; but

our Duty to our Country, our Refpect for the Reputation of the Commander-in-Chief of our Army, impel us to it ; for a Knowledge of the Force that has been required of the States for the Campaign, and which was allowed to be adequate to an important Enterprize, will induce a Belief in our Countrymen, in the World, that it has been furnifhed, and they muft ftand amazed to fee our Army inactive, and Things not in that Train for Operation which ought, in fuch a Cafe, to be expected, efpecially at this advanced Seafon of the Year.

Again : The Force of our Ally, now with us, and the fhortly expected Arrival of the Second Divifion, muft clearly evince the Utility of our Army's being put in a Condition to undertake an Enterprife which, if fuccefsful, muft give a deadly Wound to our unrelenting and ambitious Foe. But what Apology can be made if, when the Commander-in-Chief of our Army fhould be called on by the Commander of the Forces of our generous Ally, and informed he is ready to undertake with him whatever Meafures he fhall think proper to point out, he fhall be re-duced to the cruel Neceffity of acknowledging his Inability to engage in any Enterprize that can possibly redound to the Honor or Reputation of the Arms of either Nation ? Sir, the Reflection is too humiliating to be dwelt on, without the extremest Pain — nay, Horror!

You must pardon us, worthy Sir, for the Freedom with which we have now delivered our Sentiments on this truly interesting Subject. We flatter ourselves great Allowances will be made for our Situation, when we daily have before our Eyes Specimens of that Want of Energy in conducting our Affairs, which must shortly so far embarrass us as to render all future Exertions inadequate to the Attainment of those great Purposes at which we aim. America Wants not Resources. We have Men (independent of those necessary for domestic Purposes) more than sufficient to compose an Army capable of answering our most sanguinary Expectations; and our Country teems with Provisions of every Kind necessary to support them. It requires Nothing more than a proper Degree of Energy to bring them forth, to make us a happy People. This we trust, Sir, the State over which you preside will shew us no Reluctance in contributing her Aid to, by taking such decisive Measures as will, without Loss of Time, bring into the Field the Remainder of your Quota of Men that have been required for the Campaign.

The Articles of Provifions, Forage and Teams, are no lefs important than Men; but as the Committee had the Honor of addreffing you a few Days ago on the Subject of Provifions, and the other Articles being fo nearly allied with that, we will not intrude it on you at this Time.

Inclofed is a Copy of a Letter from the Commander-in-Chief of the 17th Inftant to the Committee. It will fully fhew you the State of the Army at this Time, and how great a Deficiency of Men there is, to what there ought to have been before this Day. However we hope, Sir, it will be no Difcouragement to your State in referving their utmoft Exertions for furnifhing the Remainder of their Troops, to join the Army as foon as poffible, and that the Idea of its being probably too late, before a fufficient Force can be collected to promife a fuccefsful Campaign will be totally banifhed; for Policy as well as Intereft dictate to us, to be always prepared to take Advantage of every favourable Conjuncture; and it is impoffible to fay how foon fuch a one will prefent itfelf.

The General's Letter treats this Subject in

every other Refpect fo fully, as renders it unneceffary to add more, than,

We have the Honor to be,

With great Refpect,

Your Excellency's moft obed't

and humble Servant,

In Behalf of the Committee,

JNO. MATHEWS.

The following Letter from General Arnold,
then in Command of the important Poft at Weft
Point, is inferted in this Connection, as having
Relation to the Subject under our Notice. It
prefents, fo far as our Information goes, a correct
Statement of the deftitute Condition of that
Poft, at the Time; a Subject doubtlefs of but
little real Intereft to the Writer, whofe treafon-
able Negotiations were then far advanced for the
Surrender of his Truft to the Enemy.

LETTER FROM GENERAL ARNOLD, AT WEST POINT,
TO NATHANIEL STEVENS, DEPUTY COMMISSARY OF
ISSUES.

Head-Quarters, Robinfon Houfe,
Auguft 24th, 1780.

Dear Sir,

The frefh Beef on Hand in Garrifon will be
expended To-morrow, and I am this Day in-

formed that the Army at Head-Quarters have been two Days without, fo that we cannot hope to derive further Supplies by Stoppages at King's Ferry; nor do I know of any other Means of procuring it than by your Exertions. Should you have none near at Hand, it will be neceffary that you apply to Col. Hay, the State Agent for New York, or fome of the Deputies for a prefent Provifion. In Order to enfure Succefs, I think it moft expedient to advife you to apply to his Excellency Governor Clinton on the Subject, ftating to him our Neceffity, and requefting his Orders on fome of the Agents of the State, for a Supply of Cattle until the purchafing Commif-faries fend fome, that we may not be obliged to break in upon our fmall Stock of falt Provifions.

With Sentiments of Efteem,

    I am, Dear Sir,

        Your ob't and very Humble Serv't,

            B. ARNOLD.

Nath'l Stevens, Efq.,

    D. C. Gen. Iffues.

Mainly through the Energy and Exertions of General La Fayette, on his Vifit to France in 1779, the French Court was induced to fend a refpectable Land and Naval Force to cooperate with the Americans in their War againſt the Engliſh, then the common Enemy of both. The Army was placed under the Command of Count Rochambeau, a Lieutenant General of the French Army, and the Fleet under the Chevalier de Ternay.

The Firſt Diviſion of the French Forces which arrived at Newport July 10th, confiſted of about five thouſand Land Troops and one thouſand Marines. The Troops were landed and encamped foutheaſt of the Town. Soon after their Arrival, the Britiſh Fleet under Admiral Graves appeared before Newport with a fuperior Force, and active Preparations were made in New York to forward from thence a Land Force fufficient to enfure Succefs before the Second Diviſion of the French Forces could arrive.

This Movement of the Britiſh Army was checked by an Appearance of an aggreſſive Advance of the Army under General Waſhington towards New York, then the principal Baſe of Operations of the Enemy.*

---

* The Attack on a Block Houfe at Bull's Ferry, oppofite the upper Part of Manhattan Iſland by General Wayne, although of itfelf unfuccefsful, is believed to have tended to check the Departure of the Britiſh

Such was the State of public Affairs at the Period when the Convention, noticed in the following Pages, was called. The Emergencies of the Hour demanded energetic Meaſures, and greater Sacrifices for the public Good. The Country already felt the Exhauſtion of a long and diſtreſſing War; but a ſettled Confidence in the Juſtice of their Cauſe, and its ultimate Triumph, incited the Patriots of that Day to new Efforts for the Achievement of their Purpoſe.

Copies of the Proceedings of this Convention were tranſmitted to the Governors of the ſeveral States, with a Requeſt that they ſhould be laid before their Legiſlatures, and an earneſt Hope that Action would be taken favorable to the Meaſures propoſed. The Action of the State of New York in this Regard will be found in the Appendix; and the Recommendations of the Convention appear to have been received with Approbation. In a Letter to General Waſhing-

Forces intended for this Expedition, and thus indirectly to have proved a brilliant Succeſs. The Repulſe of General Wayne from the Block Houſe became the Theme of a ſatirical Poem, written by Major André, entitled *The Cow Chace.* The tragic Fate of this young Officer, and the prophetic foreboding of his own Fate, contained in the cloſing Stanza, have given unuſual Intereſt to this Poem.

ton, dated September 1ſt, 1780, Governor Clinton
ſays:

"I take the Liberty of encloſing (confidentially)
for your Excellency's Peruſal, a Copy of the Proceedings of a Convention of Committees from
the States of Maſſachuſetts Bay, Connecticut and
New Hampſhire, in which I am happy to find,
even at this late Hour, Sentiments which, gene-
rally adopted, cannot fail of producing much
Good. I believe I may venture to aſſure you,
Sir, that as the moſt ſenſible among us have from
the Beginning of the Conteſt foreſeen the Con-
ſequences of temporary Expedients, they will
meet the cheerful Approbation of this State."

General Waſhington, in Reply, expreſſed his
Satisfaction at the Information given, and in a
Letter, addreſſed to James Bowdoin, Preſident
of the Council of Maſſachuſetts, dated Auguſt
28th, he ſays in Alluſion to this Subject:

⁂   ⁂   ⁂ "I am informed of a Set of Reſolutions lately entered into by a Convention of
Delegates from the four Eaſtern States, which,
if rightly repreſented to me, and ſhould they be
carried into Execution, will be the moſt likely
Means that could be adopted to reſcue our
Affairs from the complicated and dreadful Em-

barraffments under which they labor, and will do infinite Honor to thofe with whom they originate. I fincerely wifh they may meet with no Oppofition or Delay in their Progrefs. Our Situation is truly delicate, and demands all our Wifdom, all our Virtue, all our Energy."

PROCEEDINGS

OF A

Convention at Boston,

AUGUST, 1780.

A T a Meeting of the Committees appointed by the States of Maſſachuſetts Bay, Connecticut and New Hampſhire, convened at Boſton, on Thurſday the third day of Auguſt, in the Year of our Lord one thouſand ſeven hundred and eighty,

Preſent—

The Honble Thomas Cuſhing, Eſqr, Nathaniel Gorham, Eſqr, John Lowell, Eſqr, from the State of Maſſachuſetts Bay.

The Honble Jeſſe Root, Eſqr, from the State of Connecticut.

The Honble John Langdon, Eſqr, from the State of New Hampſhire.

The State of Rhode Iſland were notified of

the Convention, approved the Meafure, and appointed a Commiſſioner, but by fome Means he was prevented from attending.*

The Commiſſioners prefent produced their feveral Appointments and Powers, which are as follows:

STATE OF MASSACHUSETTS BAY, ⎰
   Council Chamber, July 24th, 1780. ⎱

Ordered, That the Honble Thomas Cuſhing, Efquire, Nathaniel Gorham, Efq^r, and John Lowell, Efq^r, be, and hereby are appointed to meet and confer with fuch Commiſſioners as the States of Connecticut, Rl.ode Iſland and Providence Plantations, and New Hampſhire, or either of them have, or may appoint to confult and advife on all fuch Bufinefs and Affairs as ſhall be brought under Confideration, relative to the War, and to promote and forward the moſt vigorous Exertions of the prefent Campaign, and to cultivate a good Underſtanding and procure a generous Treatment of the Officers and Men of our great and generous Ally, and make Report thereof accordingly.

   True Copy.

      Atteſt   JOHN AVERY, D. Sec'y.

---

* The Commiſſioner appointed by Rhode Iſland was the Hon. Richard Bradford. See Appendix.

STATE OF CONNECTICUT.

[L. S.]   BY THE GOVERNOR.

To Eliphalet Dyer, Esqr.

You being appointed by the Governor and Council of Safety to meet with Commiſſioner or Commiſſioners, who are or may be appointed and impowered by the States of New Hampſhire, Maſſachuſetts Bay, and Rhode Iſland and Providence Plantations, or either of them, to conſult and adviſe on the Buſineſs and Affairs neceſſary to promote and forward the moſt vigorous Exertions in the preſent Campaign, wherein theſe, with others of the United States, are called upon by the Committee of Congreſs by their Letter of the 2d of June laſt, for ſpecific Aid of Men, Proviſions, Forage, and the Means of Tranſportation ; and alſo, wherein his moſt Chriſtian Majeſty, the Illuſtrious Ally of the United States of America, hath undertaken to furniſh and aſſiſt them with Marine and Land Forces lately arrived at Newport, that there ſhould be no Failure on our Part, nor any Abuſe or Diſappointment of the Expectations and benevolent and good Intentions of our foreign Helpers, and that other Affairs relative to the War, brought under Confideration agreeable to their or your Inftructions, may be fettled and agreed upon,

Therefore, you are hereby fully inftructed, authorized and empowered, to proceed to Bofton, in the State of Maffachufetts Bay, with all convenient Speed; there to meet with fuch Commiflioners of faid States as fhall be appointed and authorized to confult and advife on all fuch Bufinefs and Affairs as fhall be brought under Confideration relative to the War, and to promote and forward the moft vigorous Exertions of the prefent Campaign, and to cultivate a good Underftanding, and procure a generous Treatment of the Officers and Men of our great and generous Ally, and make Report thereof accordingly.

Given under my Hand and Seal at Arms, this 17th Day of July, 1780.

JONTH TRUMBULL.

STATE OF CONNECTICUT.

[L. S.]   BY THE GOVERNOR.

To Jeffe Root, Efq^r.

You being appointed by the Governor and Council of Safety to meet with Commiflioners from the State of Maffachufetts, Rhode Ifland,

and Providence Plantations, and New Hampshire, in the Room of Eliphalet Dyer, Esqr :

You are hereby authorized and impowered to proceed to Boston with the same Powers, Authorities and Instructions given him the said Dyer, by his annexed Commission and Instructions, dated the 17th Instant, and to make Report.

Given under my Hand and Seal at Arms, at Lebanon, the 29th July, 1780.

JON^TH TRUMBULL.

STATE OF NEW HAMPSHIRE, }
In Committee of Safety, July 29, 1780. }

Resolved, That the Honble John Langdon, Esqr be, and hereby is appointed a Delegate for and on behalf of this State, to proceed to Boston to join with such Delegates as are or may be appointed by the States of Massachusetts Bay, Connecticut, and Rhode Island, to meet at Boston on the 2d of August next, to consult and advise in all such Business and Affairs as shall be brought under Consideration relative to the War, and to promote and forward the most vigorous Exertions of the present Campaign, and to cultivate good Understanding and procure a generous Treatment

of the Officers and Men of our great and generous Ally, or on any other Matters that may be
thought advifable for the Public Good, and to
report the Proceedings of faid Delegates to
this Committee, or the General Affembly of this
State.

In behalf of the Com^tee,

M. WEARE, Pref^d.

John Langdon, Efquire.

After Communication of the Powers as above,
the Convention made choice of the Honble
Thomas Cufhing, Efq^r, for their Prefident, and
Henry Alline as Clerk.

And they proceeded to confult and advife upon
the Means neceffary to be imployed by the
States they reprefent, to comply with the Requi-
fitions of Congrefs, and of their Committee of
Cooperation at Head-Quarters, and to carry on
and render effectual the Operations of the prefent
Campaign ; and having adjourned from Day to
Day until the ninth Day of Auguft Inftant, agreed
and refolved to recommend to their refpective
States the following Meafures :

1ft. That notwithftanding thefe States have
ordered the Number of Men required of them,

and made great Exertions to raise them, and the greater Part are already gone on to the Army, yet as the intended Operations of the present Campaign will not admit of any Diminution of the Force required, it is earnestly recommended to the several States represented in this Convention, to cause their Complement of Men to be immediately completed;

2dly. That in Order to preserve Uniformity in the Purchases in the different States aforesaid, and to prevent Irregularity and Disappointment in procuring and forwarding the Supplies to the Army;

Resolved, That it be recommended to the Supreme Executive of each State, to direct the Persons at the Head of the purchasing Department in them respectively, to correspond with each other, and as often as once every Month, to inform each other of the Purchases they have made, what they have sent on, and what they will be able to furnish in the Run of a Month, with the average Price they give.*

---

* The Advancement of Prices, on Account of the Depreciation of the Paper Currency, issued by Order of Congress and the several States, had at this Period become a most serious Difficulty in the Prosecution of the War. Towards the End of February, 1780, the New York Legis-

3dly. *Resolved*, That it be recommended to the several States aforesaid, as a Measure necessary,

lature, in a Law entitled, " An Act for the General Limitation of Prices, and to prevent engrossing and withholding within this State," fixed the legal Prices of many of the more important Commodities, as follows:

Good merchantable Wheat, - - 20 Dollars per Bushel.
Peas and White Beans, - - 20 " "
Rye, - - - - - - 13 " "
Good merchantable Indian Corn, 11 " "
"   "   Buckwheat, - 8 " "
"   "   Oats, - - 7 " "
Pork, well fatted, - - - - 89 Dollars per hundred Weight.
Best Grass fed Beef, - - 6 Shillings per Pound.
Best Stall fed Beef, in January, - 7 " "
"   "   February, - 8 " "
"   "   March, - 9 " "
"   "   April, - 10 " "
"   "   May, - - 11 " "
"   "   June, - 12 " "
Good Butter by the Firkin or Cask, 18 Shillings per Pound.
"   "   by the small Quantity, 21 " "
American Cheese, of the best Quality, 12 " "
Rendered Tallow, - - - 16 " "
"   Hog's Lard, - - 12 " "
Ram Hides, - - - - 7 " "
Good tanned Sole-Leather, - 4 Dollars "
Best Sort of Men's Shoes made from
    Neat's Leather, - - - 25 Dollars per Pair.
Men's Calf Skin Shoes, of best Quality, 28 " "

The List embraced many other Articles in common Use. Wages were not to exceed twenty Fold the Rates of 1774. Teaming was limited to a Charge of six Dollars per Mile, for every 2,000 Pounds Weight.

that they tranfport their Quota of the Supplies required to the Army, or wherever the Commander-in-Chief, or other proper Officer, fhall direct, for the prefent, and until other Means of Conveyance are provided, and charge the fame to the United States, and to give information thereof to the Commander-in-Chief, and the Committee of Cooperation.

4th. *Refolved*, That it be recommended to the feveral States, to impower the chief Officer of the American Troops ferving with the Allied Army, to take prudent Meafures to prevent any Impofition or Frauds being practiced by People bringing Provifions to Market and the Army, by extorting exorbitant Prices, or otherways, and to iffue fuch Orders from Time to Time as may have a Tendency to induce People to bring plentifully to Market, and to fell at reafonable Prices.

5th. *Refolved*, That it be recommended to the feveral States that have Acts laying an Embargo on the Tranfportation of Articles by Land from one State to another, to repeal them as being unneceffary, and tending rather to injure than ferve the Common Caufe we are engaged to fupport and maintain ; to continue Embargos on Provifions by Water, and that particular Care be taken to prevent all illicit Trade with the Enemy.*

6th. It is confidered to be of great Importance that the old Continental Bills fhould be funk, agreeable to the Refolution of Congrefs,† in Order to fupport the public Credit, and that all the States fhould adopt effectual Meafures for that Purpofe.

Therefore, *Refolved*, To recommend to our

---

* At this Period feveral of the States, under the Pretext of Rifk of Cpature by the Enemy, or to fupply the domeftic Wants of their own In-habitants, had paffed Laws forbidding the Exportation of Wheat and other ftaple Articles of Food from their Borders. The Meafure was in fome Cafes deemed arbitrary and oppreffive ; but fo far as the Prohibition extended to Tranfportation by Water, it was manifeftly proper. Perfons engaged in illicit Traffic with the Enemy often reforted to the Artifice of pretended Capture and mock Refiftance, in transferring their Commodities to or from the Enemy's Lines. Thefe Scenes were of conftant Occurrence between the Parties known as "Skinners" and "Cowboys," who infefted the Settlements on the lower Hudfon. Although oftenfibly Partizans of one or the other of the Belligerents, they deferved the Confidence of neither, and juftly deferved the Appellation of "Border Ruffians."

The New Jerfey Law, then in Force, prohibiting the Exportation of Provifions from that State, was paffed October 7, 1779.

It laid a ftrict Embargo upon the Exportation of Provifions excepting into New York, Pennfylvania and Delaware, and had for its profeffed Objects to fupply the Wants of the Army, and to diftrefs the Enemy by withholding the Supplies they might otherwife obtain by the Capture of Veffels laden with Provifions.

† See Appendix, for a Statement of the Action of Congrefs upon this Subject.

refpective States, to fink the Quota of faid Bills affigned them, by Taxation as far as poffible; and in Cafe the Whole cannot be funk within the Time limited by that Means, that the States employ fuch other effectual Meafures for the Purpofe as fhall be moft agreeable to them.*

* The Continental Bills of Credit, which had been iffued early in the Revolution, began to depreciate foon after they appeared. The Scale of Value varied fomewhat in the feveral States, and was fixed by Law, as a Bafis for the Payment of Debts contracted at different Periods. In New York, a Law paffed March 30, 1781, fpecified the Values from the 1ft of Sept., 1777, to the middle of March, 1780, at Intervals of two Weeks. The following Table exhibits thefe Values, as compared with the monthly Values as eftablifhed in Maffachufetts by a fimilar Law, paffed Sept. 29, 1780. The par Value in each Cafe was Gold and Silver. We have added a Column, fhowing the Percentage of this Value which the Bills equalled, as fpecified by the Laws of New York.

Date.	Mafs.	N. Y.	Per Cent in N. Y.
January 1, 1777,	$105	——	——
February 1, "	107	——	——
March 1, "	109	——	——
April 1, "	112	——	——
May 1, "	115	——	——
June 1, "	120	——	——
July 1, "	125	——	——
Auguft 1, "	150	——	——
September 1, "	175	$100	100.0
" 15, "	——	104	96.1
October 1, "	275	109	91.7
" 15, "	——	115	86.9
November 1, "	300	121	82.6

That each State immediately inform Congrefs
of the Meafures they have taken, which were

Date.				Mafs.	N. Y.	Per Cent in N. Y.
November 15, 1777,	-	-	-	——	$127	78.7
December 1, "	-	-	-	$310	133	75.2
" 15, "	-	-	-	——	139	71.9
January 1, 1778,	-	-	-	325	146	68.4
" 15, "	-	-	-	——	152	67.1
February 1, "	-	-	-	350	160	62.4
" 15, "	-	-	-	——	167	59.9
March 1, "	-	-	-	375	175	57.1
" 15, "	-	-	-	——	186	33.7
April 1, "	-	-	-	400	203	48.3
" 15, "	-	-	-	——	214	46.7
May 1, "	-	-	-	400	230	43.4
" 15, "	-	-	-	——	245	40.8
June 1, "	-	-	-	400	265	37.7
" 15, "	-	-	-	——	281	35.6
July 1, "	-	-	-	425	303	33.0
" 15, "	-	-	-	——	332	30.1
Auguft 1, "	-	-	-	450	348	28.7
" 15, "	-	-	-	——	370	27.0
September 1, "	-	-	-	475	400	25.0
" 15, "	-	-	-	——	429	23.3
October 1, "	-	-	-	500	464	21.6
" 15, "	-	-	-	——	500	20.0
November 1, "	-	-	-	545	545	18.3
" 15, "	-	-	-	——	584	17.1
December 1, "	-	-	-	634	634	15.7
" 15, "	-	-	-	——	679	14.7
January 1, 1779,	-	-	-	742	742	13.4
" 15, "	-	-	-	——	796	12.5

adopted in full Confidence and Expectation of the other States complying with the Reſolution

Date.		Maſs.	N. Y.	Per Cent in N. Y.
February 1, 1779, - - -		$868	$868	11.4
" 15, " - - - - -		——	932	10.7
March 1, " - - -		1,000	1,000	10.0
" 15, " - - - - -		——	1,048	9.5
April 1, " - - -		1,104	1,104	9.0
" 15, " - - - - -		——	1,156	8.7
May 1, " - - -		1,215	1,219	8.2
" 15, " - - - - -		——	1,272	7.8
June 1, " - - -		1,342	1,344	7.3
" 15, " - - - - -		——	1,404	7.1
July 1, " - - -		1,477	1,486	6.7
" 15, " - - - - -		——	1,548	6.4
Auguſt 1, " - - -		1,630	1,631	6.1
" 15, " - - - - -		——	1,709	5.8
September 1, " - - -		1,800	1,800	5.5
" 15, " - - - - -		——	1,908	5.2
October 1, " - - -		2,030	2,032	4.9
" 15, " - - - - -		——	2,151	4.6
November 1, " - - -		2,308	2,340	4.3
" 15, " - - - - -		——	2,433	4.1
December 1, " - - -		2,593	2,597	3.8
" 15, " - - - -		——	2,741	3.5
January 1, 1780, - - -		2,934	2,932	3.4
" 15, " - - - -		——	3,115	3.2
February 1, " - - -		3,322	3,333	3.0
" 15, " - - - - -		——	3,532	2.8
March 1, " - - -		3,736	3,732	2.6
" 15, " - - - - -		——	4,000	2.5
April 1, " - - -		4,000	——	——

of Congrefs, which will be rendered extenfively beneficial, only by the Cooperation of all, and may be totally defeated by the Failure of any.

7th. *Refolved,* To recommend to each of thefe States, as a neceffary Means to fupport the Credit of the new Bills, immediately to eftablifh Funds for finking, annually, at leaft one-fixth Part of the Bills they fhall emit, purfuant to the Refolution of Congrefs; and that the Tax for raifing a Fund for the firft Year be paid in Silver and Gold, or the Produce of the Country; the other five Years to be paid in Silver and Gold, or the fpecific Bills, not to be reiffued; that the Credit of the Paper Bills muft reft upon the Funds provided for their Redemption; as in our Opinion every Attempt to fupport their Credit by forcing them into Circulation tends to defeat the Purpofe, and to depreciate them.

8. *Refolved,* To recommend to the States aforefaid, not to emit any more Bills on their own particular Credit, and in no Cafe to have in Circulation at any one Time, of both State and new Continental Bills, more than the Quantity affigned them by the Refolution of Congrefs.

9. *Refolved,* That it be recommended to the States aforefaid, that whenever any Soldier or

Seaman belonging to any of the said States, passing through another State, shall fall sick and be in Want (where he cannot be conveniently sent to a public Hospital), the Selectmen and Overseers of the Poor of the Town in which he shall so fall sick, and shall take Care to Provide for him necessary Physick and nursing at the Expense of the State to which he belongs, keeping a particular Account of the Expenses, and have the same subscribed by said Soldier or Seaman, with a Certificate of the State, Town, Regiment and Company, or Vessel, to which he belongs, whenever it can be done; which Account shall be adjusted and paid in the first Instance by the State in which he fell sick, and be reimbursed by the State to which he belongs.

10th. *Resolved,* That it be recommended to the States aforesaid, to use proper Caution, to prevent any improper Articles of Intelligence being communicated to the Enemy through the Channel of Newspapers or otherways, to the Prejudice of public Measures.

11. *Resolved,* That it be recommended to the States aforesaid, that whenever any Levies of Men are called for from said States, the Men procured or hired by one State or their Subjects from

G

another, without the Licenfe of the State to which the Man belongs, fhall be counted to the Quota of the State to which he belongs, in like Manner as Soldiers raifed for the Continental Army.

12th. Although in the Opinion of this Convention, no Exertions ought to be fpared on the Part of thefe States to facilitate and carry into Execution the Meafures adopted for the prefent Campaign, yet they conceive it to be effential to our final Safety, to the Eftablifhment of public Credit, and to put a fpeedy and happy Iffue to the prefent calamitous War, that the Union of thefe States be fixed in a more folid and permanent Manner, that the Powers of Congrefs be more clearly afcertained and defined, and that the important national Concerns of the United States be under the Superintendency and Direction of one fupreme Head; that the proper Eftimates of our public Wants be feafonably made, and the neceffary Refources provided, and regularly and economically drawn forth and expended.

To that End,

Refolved, That it be recommended to the States aforefaid, to impower their Delegates in Congrefs to confederate with fuch of the States as will accede to the Confederation propofed by Congrefs,* and that they inveft their Delegates in Congrefs with Powers competent for the Government and Direction of all thofe common and national Affairs which do not, nor can come within the Jurifdiction of the particular States; and that the States aforefaid reprefent to Congrefs the Importance and Neceffity of their fo doing; that they form a permanent Syftem, eftablifhing proper Boards, Officers and Regulations for the Direction of the feveral Departments neceffary to be executed under Congrefs, to the End that proper Eftimates of the public Wants may be feafonably made, and fufficient Funds of Money provided for anfwering the fame from the States, or by foreign Loans procured on the Credit of the United States; that the Refources of the Nation may be regularly drawn forth and economically expended, and that the States be feafonably called upon for Supplies of Men and Money, for filling the public Magazines, and the Eftablifhment of an Army during the War.

13th. *Refolved,* That it be recommended to the

---

* The Articles of Confederation then pending for Adoption, were recommended by Congrefs July 9, 1778, and officially announced as adopted in March, 1781. Congrefs met under this Authority on the 2d of March of that Year. The laft State acceding to the Arrangement was Maryland

States aforefaid, to requeft of Congrefs, in Order to prevent fuch Embarraffments and Expence as the States have labored under in furnifhing Supplies for the prefent Campaign, happening again, that effectual Means be immediately employed to fill the public Magazines, and to raife Men to fill the Continental Battalions for the War by the 18th of January next,—And it is further recommended, that in Cafe the War continues, and Congrefs fhould not take Meafures for the Purpofe, and notify the States aforefaid by the firft of November next, that the faid States do at all Events furnifh their Quota of Men and Provifions, and charge the fame to the United States, and to procure Uniformity in the Meafures that may be neceffary to be taken by thefe States in common with each other; this Convention recommend a Meeting of Commiffioners from the feveral States, to be held at Hartford on the 2d Wednefday of November next, and invite the State of New York and others to join them that fhall think proper.

Refolved, That the Proceedings of this Convention be fent to the States of Rhode Ifland and New York, with a Letter from the Prefident, defiring their Concurrence in the Meafures agreed upon, if they approve thereof.

THOMAS CUSHING, Prefident.

APPENDIX.

RHODE ISLAND.

THE following Correſpondence and Proceedings, from Vol. IX, of the *Rhode Iſland Colonial Records*, ſhow the Part taken by that State in the Convention at Boſton in Auguſt, 1780.

LETTER FROM GOVERNOR TRUMBULL OF CONNECTICUT TO THE GOVERNOR OF RHODE ISLAND.

Lebanon, 14th July, 1780.

Sir,

The late Arrangement of our public Affairs, the diſconcerted State of the Commiſſary Department, the large Demands upon the New England States for Supplies for the Army, and the regular Manner in which theſe Supplies ought to be furniſhed, eſpecially of freſh Proviſions, ſo as to prevent a Want at one Time, or a Surplus at another, the large Demands for the Army and Navy of our Ally, which are now arrived, to be fupplied by thefe States, as fuch as alfo the Market, which, by their Arrival, will be opened for a Variety of Articles to be fupplied by Individuals; not only to prevent a Difappointment of their Expectations in their Supplies, but of their being impofed and extorted upon by extravagant Prices by Individuals, which may greatly endanger a Difaffection, and many other Matters of general Concern in this important Conjuncture of our Affairs—calls for a Union of Councils and Meafures.

To effect which, with the greateft Expedition, we have thought it neceffary to fend one of our Board to meet fuch Gentlemen as may be appointed from the States of Rhode Ifland, Maffachufetts and New Hampfhire, or fuch of them as fhall concur in the Meafure, at Bofton, as early next Week as poffible, to confer on thefe and other important Subjects peculiarly neceffary at this Day; to agree upon and adopt fuch fimilar Meafures as may be moft conducive to the general Intereft.

We have forwarded this Intimation by an Exprefs to the Council of War, at Providence; and if agreeable to them, it is requefted they would unite in their requeft with ours, to the Council of War at Bofton, by them immediately to be communicated to the Prefident and Council in New Hampfhire, for the Purpofe that fuch Convention may be held at Bofton with all poffible

Expedition. The Reasons for this Proposal are so obvious, the Matters so pressing, that we apprehend no Apology need be made for this Application.

I am, with Esteem and Regard, Sir,
Your obedient, humble Servant,
JON'TH TRUMBULL.

To his Excellency
Governor Greene.

LETTER FROM THE GOVERNOR OF RHODE ISLAND TO GOVERNOR TRUMBULL OF CONNECTICUT.

Newport, July 19, 1780.

Sir,

I was, on the 17th Instant, favored with yours of the 14th, and I have laid the same before the General Assembly at the present Session.

They are fully impressed with the Necessity and Propriety of the Measure proposed, and have requested me to inform you that they will appoint a Committee to attend at Boston, for the Purpose mentioned in your Letter on Wednesday, the 26th Day of July Instant. I shall immediately communicate this Resolution to the President of the Council of Massachusetts Bay.

The General Assembly being sincerely desirous of accommodating the Officers of the Army and Navy of his most Christian Majesty, now at this Place, and of furnishing them with the necessary

Supplies, have paffed a Refolution, a Copy whereof at their Requeft I now enclofe you. I muft requeft your Attention to this Refolution, and that you would be pleafed to grant Permiffion for the Purpofe therein mentioned, as it will be otherwife impracticable to procure the neceffary Supply of Flour.

I am, with Efteem and Regard, Sir,
Your obedient, humble Servant,
WILLIAM GREENE.

To his Excellency
Governor Trumbull.

LETTER FROM THE GOVERNOR OF RHODE ISLAND TO THE PRESIDENT OF THE COUNCIL OF MASSACHU-SETTS.

Newport, July 20, 1780.

Sir,

A Letter of the 14th Inftant from Governor Trumbull, propofing a Committee from each of the New England States, to convene at Bofton, to confer on very important Meafures therein propofed, I laid before the General Affembly of this State, which unanimoufly concurred with the Propofal; and have requefted me to write you, recommending the Concurrence of your State with the fame; and if agreeable, to requeft you to write to the Prefident and Council of New Hampfhire on this neceffary Meafure.

It is propofed to convene at Bofton, on Wednefday, the 26th Day of July inftant.

I am, with Efteem and Regard, Sir,
Your obedient Servant,
WILLIAM GREENE.

To the honorable Prefident of the
Council of Maffachufetts Bay.

PROCEEDINGS OF THE GENERAL ASSEMBLY FOR THE
STATE OF RHODE ISLAND AND PROVIDENCE PLANT-
ATIONS, AT NEWPORT,

On the third Monday in July, 1780.

His Excellency William Greene, Governor.

The Hon. William Weft, Deputy Governor.

✳ ✳ ✳ " It is voted and refolved, that Metcalf
Bowler, Thomas Rumreill and Jofeph Stanton,
Jr., Efqs., be, and they are hereby appointed a
Committee to draught an Anfwer to a Letter
from Governor Trumbull, requefting the Appointment of a Perfon to meet the Deputies from
the New England States, at Bofton, for the Purpofes in the faid Letter mentioned; and that the
faid Committee alfo draught a Letter to the
Prefident of the Council of the Commonwealth
of Maffachufetts, requefting them to concur in
the Meafures propofed."

✳ ✳ ✳ " Whereas, his Excellency, Governor
Trumbull, hath informed this Affembly that a

H

Commiffioner is appointed by the State of Connecticut, to meet Commiffioners from the other
States in New England, in a Convention, to be
holden at Bofton for the Purpofe of agreeing upon
the Mode of furnifhing the neceffary Supplies
from the faid States for the prefent Campaign,
and upon fuch other Meafures as may tend to
promote the Succefs of the allied Armies, and
requefted this State to appoint a Commiffioner
for the aforefaid Purpofes; and this Affembly
being convinced that the Meafures propofed will
be effentially beneficial to the United States,—

"Do vote and refolve, and it is voted and
refolved, that the Honorable William Bradford,
Efq., be, and he is hereby appointed a Commiffioner on the Part of this State, to meet the
Commiffioners from the other States in New
England, in the faid Convention; that he be,
and hereby is, empowered to agree to fuch Meafures as the faid Convention, or the major Part
thereof, fhall judge neceffary to be adopted by
the faid States in New England, in the prefent
important Crifis of the public Affairs; and that
he make Report of the Refolutions of the faid
Convention to this Affembly for Ratification."

ADDRESS OF THE GENERAL ASSEMBLY OF RHODE
ISLAND TO GENERAL ROCHAMBEAU.

The Reprefentatives of the State of Rhode
Ifland and Providence Plantations, in General
Affembly convened, with the moft pleafing
Satisfaction, take the earlieft Opportunity of
congratulating Compte De Rochambeau, Lieu-
tenant-General of the Army of His Moft Chriftian
Majefty, upon his fafe Arrival within the United
States. Upon this Occafion, we cannot be too
expreffive of the grateful Senfe we entertain of
the generous and magnanimous Aid afforded
to the United States by their illuftrious Friend
and Ally. Sufficient had been the Proofs of his
Zeal and Friendfhip; the prefent Inftance muft
conftrain even envious, difcontented Britons to
venerate the Wifdom of his Councils, and the
Sincerity of his noble Mind. We look forward
with a moft pleafing Expectation to the End of
a Campaign, in which the allied Force of France
and thefe United States, under the Smiles of
Divine Providence, may be productive of Peace
and Happinefs to the contending Powers, and
Mankind in general. We affure you, Sir, our
Expectations are enlarged, when we confider the
Wifdom of His Moft Chriftian Majefty in your
Appointment, as the Commander of his Army
deftined to our Affiftance. Be affured, Sir, of
every Exertion in the Power of this State to
afford the neceffary Refrefhments to the Army

under your Command, and to render the Service to all Ranks as agreeable and happy as it is honorable.

We are, in Behalf of the General Aſſembly,
The General's moſt obedient and
Moſt devoted, humble Servants,
WILLIAM GREENE,
WILLIAM BRADFORD.

To Lieutenant General
Compte De Rochambeau.

REPLY OF GENERAL ROCHAMBEAU TO THE ADDRESS OF THE GENERAL ASSEMBLY OF RHODE ISLAND.

Gentlemen:— The King, my Maſter, hath ſent me to the Aſſiſtance of his good and faithful Allies, the United States of America. At preſent, I only bring over the Van-guard of a much greater Force, deſtined for their Aid; and the King has ordered me to aſſure them, that his whole power ſhall be exerted for their Support.

The French Troops are under the ſtricteſt Diſcipline; and, acting under the Orders of General Waſhington, will live with the Americans as their Brethren; and Nothing will afford me greater Happineſs than Contributing to their Succeſs.

I am highly ſenſible of the Marks of Reſpect ſhown me by the General Aſſembly, and beg leave to aſſure them that, as Brethren, not only my Life, but the Lives of the Troops under my Command, are entirely devoted to their Service.

(Signed)   The COUNT DE ROCHAMBEAU.

The following is a perfect Lift of the French Fleet under the Chevalier De Ternay, now at Rhode Ifland :

The French Fleet at Rhode Ifland.

SHIPS' NAMES.	GUNS.	MEN.	COMMANDERS.
Le Duc De Bourgogne,	84	1,200	Admiral De Ternay.
Le Neptune, - - -	74	700	Deftouches.
Le Conquerant, - -	74	700	
L'Eveille, - - -	64	600	De Tribiand.
Le Province, - -	64	600	C. B. De Mefigny.
Ardent (olim Britifh), -	64	600	
Le Jafon, - - -	64	600	
La Fantafque, ferving as a Hofpital Ship.			

FRIGATES.

La Surveillante, - -	40	300	De Caillet.
L'Andromaque, - -	36	250	De Ronevel.
La Sibelle, - - -	36	250	Bar De Clugney.
La Hermoine, - -	36	250	De la Touche.
Pelican, American Veffel,	29	160	

ARMED SHIPS.

Le Bruen, - - -	——	——	Des Arros.
La Complafe, -	——	——	De Noulds.

The land Forces confift of—

Regiment de Bourbonnois.	Regiment de Soiffonois.
" Royal Deux Ponts.	Legion de Laufun.
" Saintonge.	Firft Battalion of Artillery.

The Frigates are to go out on a Cruife.

ADDRESS OF THE GENERAL ASSEMBLY OF RHODE ISLAND TO CHEVALIER DE TERNAY.

The Reprefentatives of the State of Rhode Ifland and Providence Plantations, in General

Affembly convened, with the moft pleafing Satif-
faction take this, the earlieft Opportunity, of
teftifying the Sentiments that are impreffed upon
them, by the great Attention which His Moft
Chriftian Majefty has invariably manifefted to
the United States. The formidable Armaments
heretofore fent to our Aid, have effentially pro-
moted our Happinefs and Independence; but at
a Time when Europe is involved in the Calamities of War by the ambitious Views of the Britifh
Court, we cannot exprefs the Gratitude we feel
upon your Arrival, with the Fleet under your
Command, deftined by our illuftrious Ally to the
Affiftance of the United States. We entreat you,
on this Occafion, to accept the warmeft Congratu-
lations of the General Affembly of the State of
Rhode Ifland and the Providence Plantations;
and be affured, Sir, of every Exertion in their
Power to afford the neceffary Refrefhments to
the Fleet, and to render the Service as agreeable and happy as it is honorable.

We are, in behalf of the General Affembly,
The Admiral's moft obedient and
Moft humble Servants,
WILLIAM GREENE,
WILLIAM BRADFORD.*

To De Chevalier Ternay.

---

* Mr. Bradford was at this Time Speaker of the Lower Houfe. The
Addrefs was prefented by a Committee, confifting of the Hon. William
Bradford, Efq., John I. Clark, Efq., Mr. Jofeph Brown, William Chan-
ning, Robert Elliott, Metcalf Bowler, and William Richmen l, Efq.

NEW YORK.

Governor Clinton, of New York, with his Meſſage at the opening of the fourth Seſſion (Auguſt 4, 1780), tranſmitted to the Legiſlature the Proceedings of the Boſton Convention, concerning which he remarked as follows:

* ⁂ * "Notwithſtanding the Meaſures hitherto purſued, and although theſe States thro' the Indulgence of Heaven abound with Proviſions, the Army has not yet received ſeaſonable and competent Supplies. I now communicate to you by Letter from the Committee of Congreſs at Head-Quarters, and the Commander-in-Chief,* upon this intereſting Subject, and recommend them to your ſerious Attention, with the fulleſt Confidence that Nothing will be wanting on your Part, and that as far as the Ability of this State extends, no Means will be left uneſſayed, to prevent the Misfortunes which muſt inevitably reſult from a Failure in the eſſential Article of Subſiſtence.

" *Gentlemen,* When we reflect upon the Situation of our public Affairs, it is evident our Embarraſſments in the Proſecution of the War are chiefly to be attributed to a Defect of Power in thoſe who ought to exerciſe a ſupreme Direction; for while Congreſs only recommend, and the different States deliberate upon the Propriety of

* Theſe Letters are given in the Introduction,

the Recommendation, we cannot expect a Union of Force or Council. From this Conviction, I take the Liberty of submitting to you whether further Means ought not to be devised for accelerating the proposed Confederation, and thereby vesting Congress with such Authority as that in all Matters which relate to the War, their Requisitions may be peremptory. It is with Pleasure I find this to have been the Sentiment of a Convention of Committees from three States, lately held at Boston, whose Proceedings, at their Request, I now lay before you."

The Senate, in their Answer to the Governor's Speech, said :

* * * "The Information your Excellency has communicated from the Committee of Congress at Head-Quarters, and from the Commander-in-Chief, relative to a Supply of Provisions is so interesting and important that it will claim our immediate Attention.

"Convinced from Experience that the Want of adequate and defined Powers in the directing Council of the Empire has been productive of much Embarrassment in prosecuting the War, induced the Necessity of partial Exertions from some States, and much beyond their just Proportion, prevented the Union of Force or Council, so essential to the Weal of the Confederacy, and evidently protracted the War ; we will, with great Alacrity, attempt to devise Means, or concur in any which will conduce to accelerate the completion of such a Confederation as will confer on

Congrefs competent Authority to draw from each Member of the Union its Proportion of Aid for the Common Caufe; and that in all Meafures which relate to the War, their Requifitions may be peremptory. The Proceedings of the Convention lately held at Bofton, and communicated to us by your Excellency, affords us a happy Prefage that the Neceflity of confirming, extending and defining the Powers of Congrefs will pervade the Whole."

EXTRACT FROM THE NEW YORK SENATE JOURNAL.

September 8, 1780.

"A Meflagè from the Honorable the Houfe of Affembly, by Mr. Benfon and Mr. Dunfcomb, was received, with the following Refolution for Concurrence, viz:

"*In Affembly*, September 7, 1780.

"*Refolved* (if the Honorable the Senate concur herein), That a Joint Committee of both Houfes of the Legiflature be appointed, to confider of the Proceedings of the Committees appointed by the States of Maffachufetts Bay, Connecticut and New Hampfhire, convened at Bofton in Auguft laft, and Report therein; and that in cafe of fuch Concurrence Mr. L'Hommedieu, Mr. Benfon, and Mr. Tayler, be of the faid Joint Committee on the Part of this Houfe.

I

" *Refolved,* That this Senate do concur with the Honorable the Houfe of Affembly in their faid Refolution, and that Mr. Schuyler, Mr. Roofevelt, and Mr. Platt, be of the faid Joint Committee on the Part of this Senate."

" *In Senate,* Sept. 22, 1780.

* * * "Mr. Benfon, from the Joint Committee of the Senate and Affembly, to whom was referred the Proceedings of the Committees appointed by the States of Maffachufetts Bay, Connecticut and New Hampfhire (convened in Bofton in Auguft laft), reported: That in the Opinion of the faid Committee, Commiffioners ought to be appointed on the Part of this State to meet Commiffioners from other States in a Convention, propofed to be held at Hartford on the fecond Wednefday in November next, and that the Committee had prepared a Draft of In-ftructions for the Commiffioners to be appointed for this State."

This Report was accepted; and on the 26th of September, Philip Schuyler, John Slofs Hobart, and Egbert Benfon were appointed Commiffioners to reprefent the State of New York in the pro-pofed Convention at Hartford.

UNITED STATES BILLS OF CREDIT.

FINANCIAL RESOLUTIONS OF CONGRESS.

The financial Subject, alluded to on Page 44, is embodied in the following Action of Congreſs on the 2d of January, 1779.

"The Board of Treaſury having, purſuant to Orders, ſelected from the Journals the Reſolutions reſpecting the calling in certain Emiſſions, and providing a Fund for ſinking the Bills of Credit emitted by Congreſs, and prepared a preamble thereto, reported the ſame; and ſundry verbal Amendments being made in the Reſolutions, the Whole was agreed to as follows:

Whereas, Theſe United States, unprovided with Revenues, and not heretofore in a Condition to raiſe them, have, in the Courſe of the preſent War, repeatedly been under the Neceſſity of emitting Bills of Credit, for the Redemption of which, the Faith of theſe United States has been ſolemnly pledged, and the Credit of which their Honor and Safety, as well as Juſtice, is highly concerned to ſupport and eſtabliſh; and *whereas,* to this End, it is eſſentially neceſſary to aſcertain the Periods of their Redemption, and ſeaſonably to eſtabliſh Funds which, in due Time, without diſtreſſing the People, ſhall make adequate Proviſion for the ſame; and *whereas,* in appointing the Payments for the ſaid Fund, it is expedient that an extra Sum be called for the current Year, both on Account of the prefent Eafe of paying it, and to reduce the Surplus in Circulation; therefore,

" *Refolved,* That thefe United States be called on to pay in their refpective Quotas of 15,000,000 Dollars for the Year 1779, and of 6,000,000 of Dollars annually for 18 Years, from and after the Year 1779, as a Fund for finking the Emiffions and Loans of thefe United States to the 31ft of December, 1778, inclufive:

"That if the Continuance and Circumftances of the War fhall make any further Emiffions neceffary for the Year enfuing, they fhall be funk in the Manner and within the Period aforefaid:

"That any of the Bills emitted by Order of Congrefs, prior to the Year 1780, and no others, be received in Payment of the faid Quotas:

"That the Bills received on the faid Quotas, except thofe for the Year 1779, be applied firft for the Payment of the Intereft, and fecondly, for the principal of Loans made by thefe United States prior to the Year 1780, and that the Refidue, together with thofe received on the Quotas of the Year 1779, be not reiffued but burned and deftroyed, as Congrefs fhall direct."

The Iffue of May 20, 1777, and April 11, 1778, having been extenfively counterfeited and circulated by the Enemy, it was refolved that they fhould be firft taken out of the Circulation; and for this Purpofe, they were made receivable for Debts and Taxes into the Continental Treafury,

and into the State Treafuries, for Continental
Taxes, until the firft of June following. They
were, alfo, to be received into the Continental
Loan Offices, and for Exchange for indented Cer-
tificates.

The Quotas of the 15,000,000 of Dollars to
be raifed by Taxes in 1779, was affigned as follows:

New Hampfhire, - - - -	$500,000
Maffachufetts Bay, - - -	2,000,000
Rhode Ifland and Providence Planta-	
tions, - - - - -	300,000
Connecticut, - - - -	1,700,000
New York, - - - - -	800,000
New Jerfey, - - - -	800,000
Pennfylvania, - - - -	1,900,000
Delaware, - - - -	150,000
Maryland, - - - - -	1,560,000
Virginia, - - - - -	2,400,000
North Carolina, - - - -	1,090,000
South Carolina, - - -	1,800,000
Georgia, - - - - -	0,000,000
	$15,000,000

On the 7th of October, 1779, the Committee,
appointed to apportion the Quotas of the refpective States, brought in a Report; whereupon it
was refolved, that the Quotas of the feveral States
to make up the monthly Affeffment of 15,000,000
Dollars, to be paid the firft Day of February
next, on the firft Day of each fucceeding Month,

to the firſt Day of October next, incluſive, as follows:

New Hampſhire, - - - -	$400,000
Maſſachuſetts Bay, - - -	2,300,000
Rhode Iſland, &c., - - -	200,000
Connecticut, - - - -	1,700,000
New York, - - - - -	750,000
New Jerſey, - - - -	900,000
Pennſylvania, - - - -	2,300,000
Delaware, - - - -	170,000
Maryland, - - - - -	1,580,000
Virginia, - - - - -	2,500,000
North Carolina, - - - -	1,000,000
South Carolina, - - -	1,200,000

$15,000,000

Georgia, being invaded, is hereafter to raiſe its Proportion.

RESOLUTIONS IN CONGRESS.

Passed March 18, 1780.

Theſe United States having been driven into this juſt and neceſſary War, at the Time when no regular civil Governments were eſtabliſhed, of ſufficient Energy to enforce the Collection of Taxes, or to provide Funds for the Redemption of ſuch Bills of Credit as their Neceſſities obliged them to iſſue; and before the Powers of Europe were ſufficiently convinced of the Juſtice of their Caufe, or of the probable Event of the Controverfy, to afford them Aid or Credit, in Confequence of which, their Bills increafing in ' Quantity beyond the Sum neceffary for the Pur- pofe of a circulating, Medium, and wanting, at the fame Time, fpecific Funds to reft on for their Redemption, they have feen them daily fink in Value, notwithftanding every Effort that has been made to fupport the fame; infomuch that they are now paffed, by common Confent, in moft Parts of thefe United States, at leaft 39-40ths below their nominal Value, and ftill remain in a State of Depreciation, whereby the Community fuffers great Injuftice, the public Finances are deranged, and the neceffary Difpofitions for the Defence of the Country are much impeded and perplexed; and *whereas*, effectually to remedy thefe Evils, for which Purpofe the United States are now become Competent, their Dependency being well affured, their civil Governments ef- tablifhed and vigorous, and the Spirit of their Citizens ardent for Exertion, it is neceffary fpeedily to reduce the Quantity of the Paper Medium in Circulation, and to eftablifh and appropriate Funds that fhall enfure the punctual Redemption of the Bills; therefore,

Refolved, That the feveral States continue to bring into the Continental Treafury by Taxes or otherwife their full Quotas of 15,000,000 Dollars monthly, as affigned to them by the Refolution of the 7th of October, 1779; a Claufe in the Refolution of the 23d of February, for relinquifhing two-thirds of the faid Quotas, to the contrary notwithftanding; and that the States be further called on to make Provifion for continuing to bring into the faid Treafury their like Quotas monthly, to the Month of April, 1781, inclufive:

That Silver and Gold be receivable in Payment of the faid Quotas, at the Rate of one Spanifh milled Dollar in lieu of 40 Dollars of the Bills now in Circulation:

That the faid Bills, as paid in, except for the Months of January and February paft, which may be neceffary for the Difcharge of paft Contracts, be not reiffued, but deftroyed:

That as faft as the faid Bills fhall be brought in to be deftroyed, and Funds fhall be eftablifhed as hereinafter mentioned, for other Bills, other Bills be iffued, not to exceed, on any Account, one-twentieth Part of the nominal Sum of the Bills brought to be deftroyed:

That the Bills which fhall be iffued be redeemable in Specie within fix Years after the prefent, and bear an Intereft at the Rate of five per centum per annum, to be paid alfo in Specie at the Redemption of the Bills, on, at the Election of the Holder, annually, at the refpective Continental Loan-Offices, in Sterling Bills of Exchange, drawn by the United States on their Commiffioners in Europe at 4f 6d Sterling per Dollar:

That the faid new Bills iffue on the Funds of individual States, for that Purpofe eftablifhed, and be figned by Perfons appointed by them, and that the Faith of the United States be alſo pledged for the Payment of the ſaid Bills, in Caſe any State on whoſe Funds they ſhall be emitted ſhould, by the Events of War, be rendered incapable to re-deem them ; which undertaking of the United States, and that of drawing Bills of Exchange for Payment of Intereſt as aforeſaid, ſhall be endorſed on the Bills to be emitted and ſigned by a Com-miſſioner to be appointed by Congreſs for that Purpoſe :

That the Face of the Bills to be emitted read as follows, viz :

The Poſſeſſor of this Bill ſhall be paid Spaniſh milled Dollars, by the 31ſt of December, 1786, with Intereſt in like Money, at the Rate of five per cent per annum, by the State of , according to an Act of the Legiſlature of the ſaid State, of the Day of , 1780 :

And the Endorſement ſhall be as follows, viz :

The United States enſure the Payment of the within Bill, and will draw Bills of Exchange for the Intereſt annually, if demanded, according to a Reſolution of Congreſs of the 18th Day of March, 1780 :

That the ſaid new Bills ſhall be ſtruck under the Direction of the Board of Treaſury, in due Proportion for each State, according to their ſaid monthly Quotas, and lodged in the Continental Loan-Offices in the reſpective States, where the Commiſſioner to be appointed by Congreſs, in Conjunction with ſuch Perſons as the reſpective States appoint, ſhall attend the ſigning of the ſaid

K

Bills; which fhall be completed no fafter than in the aforefaid Proportion of one to twenty of the other Bills brought in to be deftroyed, and which fhall be lodged for that Purpofe in the faid Loan-Offices:

That as the faid new Bills are figned and completed, the States refpectively, on whofe Funds they iffue, receive fix-tenths of them, and that the Remainder be fubject to the Orders of the United States, and credited to the States on whofe Funds they are iffued, the Accounts whereof fhall be adjufted agreeably to the Refolution of Oct. 6, 1779:

That the faid new Bills be receivable in Payment of the faid monthly Quotas, at the fame Rate as aforefaid of Specie; the Intereft thereon to be computed to the refpective States, to the Day the Payment becomes due:

That the refpective States be charged with fuch Parts of the Intereft on their faid Bills as fhall be paid by the United States in Bills of Exchange; and the Accounts thereof fhall be adjufted agreeably to the Refolution aforefaid, of the 6th of October, 1779:

That whenever Intereft on the Bills to be emitted fhall be paid prior to their Redemption, fuch Bills fhall be thereupon exchanged for others of the like Tenor, to bear Date from the Expiration of the Year for which fuch Intereft is paid:

That the feveral States be called on to provide Funds for their Quota of the faid new Bills, to be fo productive as to fink or redeem one-fixth

Part of them annually, after the firſt Day of January next:

That Nothing in the foregoing Reſolution ſhall be conſtrued to aſcertain the Proportions of the Expenſe incurred by the War, which each State on a final Adjuſtment ought to be charged with, or to exclude the Claims of any State to have the Prices at which different States have furniſhed Supplies for the Army hereafter taken into Conſideration and equitably adjuſted:

That the foregoing Reſolutions, with a Letter from the Preſident, be deſpatched to the Executive of the ſeveral States, and that they be requeſted to call their Aſſemblies, if not already convened, as ſpeedily as poſſible to take them into immediate Conſideration, and to eſtabliſh ample and certain Funds for the Purpoſes therein mentioned, and to take every other Meaſure neceſſary to carry the ſame into full and vigorous Effect; and they tranſmit their Acts for that Purpoſe to Congreſs without Delay.

The Legiſlature of New York, on the 4th of March, 1779, paſſed an Act to call out of Circulation the Iſſues of May 20, 1777, and April 11, 1778, by requiring them to be paid into the Continental Loan-Office for exchange. On the 6th of March, 1780, this State, as a further Meaſure in Support of the public Credit, paſſed "An Act for raiſing the Sum of 5,000,000 of

Dollars by Tax within this State, and for other Purpofes therein mentioned."

This Act provided for Tax upon the feveral Counties of 3,000,000 of Dollars, to be paid on the 1ft of April, and 2,000,000 by the 1ft of July.

In New Jerfey, this Meafure was met by the Paffage of an Act, on the 8th of June, 1779, entitled " An Act to raife the Sum of one Million of Pounds in the State of New Jerfey." It provided for an Affeffment upon the Perfons and Property of the Inhabitants; and the Powers and Duties of the Officers charged with carrying the Law into Effect were prefcribed in Detail.

FINIS

INDEX.